Loss De Plott

The Colour
Blue

Stephan J Myers

Published by Hershey Reese & Myers Ltd 2014

First published in Great Britain in 2014 by
Hershey Reese & Myers Limited
Reg. No. 7331321

A CIP catalogue record for this book is available
from the British Library

Paperback (colour) ISBN **978-0-9927274-4-4**

For promises made that must never be broken.

The Colour Blue

It may well be, that you have read, the strangest tale of the colour red.

The oddest tale, about a book of dreams, where nothing inside is as it seems.

A gift to Loss from a man wearing red, not his coat or his shoes, but the hat on his head.

And now we must talk of the colour blue, for much you must learn and know to be true.

A curious colour not at all like red, where the things that you see must stay in your head.

This colour to be found in a book of dreams, where the words that are written are not what they seem.

A book in which you can draw or write, when you wake from your sleep at the end of the night.

Pictures of places far away, where sometimes Loss would stop and play.

Places to be found when asleep
in her bed, but never to be
drawn in the colour red.

There were snowmen who
danced and played all night,
they really were the most
curious sight.

Yet stranger still was a boy
wearing blue, who told her a tale
and swore it was true.

The oddest boy you have ever
seen, with hair of straw and eyes
of green.

A hat of felt upon his head, with coat of blue and stars of red.

Twigs for fingers, hair of moss, he seemed to Loss to be very cross.

And so it was with his story begun, they sat together in the midday sun.

"It was on the eve of Halloween, when witches and ghouls are often seen.

Lanterns burning, broomsticks and spells; all the things you know so well.

With my parents sleeping by the fireside, I opened the door and she saw inside.

'Trick or treat,' she said to me and held out her hands for me to see.

One was closed, her fist held tight, in the other a pen the colour of night.

The strangest blue you might ever see and the treat I chose, from her to me.

But shaking her head she looked very sad and I wondered then if I had done something bad.

Then holding it out for me to take, she asked of me a promise to make.

'Write the tale of All Hallow's Eve, for the magic is real for those who believe'

It was with these words she said goodbye and upon her broomstick I saw her fly.

Laughing aloud as she flew by the moon, she cast a spell that changed that room.

Spiders spinning webs of red; black bats flying about my head.

The pumpkin grew legs and danced about; the skeleton shook and was heard to shout.

'Whatever you promise be sure to do and write what you see in the colour blue!'

But later that night when my parents woke, they thought my pen in blue a joke.

Saying witches and ghouls were all in my head, they took my pen and sent me to bed.

Now truth be told I was slow to sleep, for the promise I made I had yet to keep.

I thought of that witch with eyes of blue, but did not know what I could do.

Pulling my cover above my head, it was the deepest blue with stars of red.

I tossed and turned the whole night long and when I woke found much was wrong.

My room was gone and I sat outside; the sky above seemed very wide.

Fireworks flying above my head, some in green, some gold, some red.

And all about me were men of straw; I counted three or maybe four.

Come with us I heard them say, but Loss I said no, for I wanted to stay.

All alone in my coat of blue, waiting for someone just like you.

Someone who could see beyond my face and knew I came from another place.

A room with a bed, a window and a door; how I long to be as I was before.

But first to be found is that pen of blue and Loss there is much I must ask of you.

When you wake and get out of bed, draw me first in the colour red.

I know this is something you should not do, but later you must write with a pen of blue.

For just like you I have a book of dreams, where nothing inside is as it seems.

Then make a lantern to be hung by your door, just like I did the year before.

Hang spiders, bats and skeletons too and wait for that witch with eyes of blue."

And so Loss woke at the end of the night, with a promise made to put things right.

She drew him in red, hung that lantern too and told her Gran what she had to do.

Sitting by the fire to warm their feet, they thought of that witch who would trick or treat.

And when the witch asked, Little Loss chose blue, for to her promise she would be true.

Now you may be thinking the witch flew away, but there was something to Loss that she had to say.

"You see, blue eyed witches are not at all bad and the pen that he lost made me very sad.

For the magic in blue keeps the darkness away, when gremlins and ghouls come out to play.

On that night of the year when fireworks fly and bonfires bright light the evening sky.

And to make it work all he had to do, was write what he saw in the colour blue.

Now Loss, when you woke, you drew in red, but there is more you must do before going to bed.

Make me a promise you will write in blue, all that you see and all that you do."

It was then Loss knew there were rules unspoken; that promises made must never be broken.

And later that night when she went to bed, she wrote in blue all the things in her head.

She wrote for that boy who was made of straw and when she stopped she began to draw.

Goblins and ghouls, black cats and more; wishing him to be as he was before.

Hoping to find him again when she slept; to tell of the promise that she had kept.

Tossing and turning to the tick of the clock, when at last she slept, she awoke to a knock.

Outside her door was a boy without blue, who had told her a tale and swore it was true.

THE END.

A Message From Stephan

I truly hope you enjoyed The Colour Blue and are looking forward to reading The Colour Gold, where Loss finds the greatest treasure of all. Of course, there is also The Colour Red, Just Ted, The Prayer and Loss De Plott, a fable for grownups who believe it is never too late to change!

You can find out a little more about the books at www.LossDePlott.com

Till next time, Stephan.

Printed in Great Britain
by Amazon.co.uk, Ltd.,
Marston Gate.